Down

Norah McClintock

orca soundings

Orca Book Publishers

Library and Archives Canada Cataloguing in Publication

McClintock, Norah
Down / written by Norah McClintock.

(Orca soundings)
ISBN 978-1-55143-768-2 (bound)
ISBN 978-1-55143-766-8 (pbk.)

I. Title.
PS8575.C62D69 2007 jC813'.54 C2007-903839-5

Summary: After serving time for assault, Remy must learn to control his anger.

First published in the United States, 2007
Library of Congress Control Number: 2007930413

Orca Book Publishers gratefully acknowledges the support for its publishing programs provided by the following agencies: the Government of Canada through the Book Publishing Industry Development Program and the Canada Council for the Arts, and the Province of British Columbia through the BC Arts Council and the Book Publishing Tax Credit.

Cover design by Teresa Bubela
Cover photography by Getty Images

Orca Book Publishers
PO Box 5626, Station B
Victoria, BC Canada
V8R 6S4

Orca Book Publishers
PO Box 468
Custer, WA USA
98240-0468

www.orcabook.com
Printed and bound in Canada.
Printed on 100% PCW recycled paper.
11 10 09 08 • 5 4 3 2

To H.B. and D.R.—Down a dead-end street.

Chapter One

I'm back about three days when I run into Asia. She's across the street with her friend Lissa. They're talking. Lissa says something, and Asia laughs. Then she turns her head and sees me.

I'm just standing there staring at her. She looks even prettier than I remember, which is really something because Asia's one of those girls who belongs in a magazine, she's that beautiful. You don't even notice her hand—at least, I don't. Her brown eyes meet mine, and her whole face changes. She looks surprised to see me. Well, why not? I only wrote to her twice—once almost as soon as I went away and once more after I got her first letter. After that, she kept writing, but I stopped reading. I didn't read any letters from anyone, not that many people wrote to me. What was the point of reading letters? They would just tell me about stuff that was happening without me. It would be like no one even missed me or noticed I was gone. Finally the letters from Asia stopped. But they probably wouldn't have if I'd written back.

And now there she is, looking across the street at me, surprised, and then—boy, it's a miracle—she smiles at me. Lissa doesn't smile, though. Lissa glowers at me and says something to Asia. She shakes her head when Asia runs across the street toward me.

"Remy," she says, breathless. "I thought I was seeing things. No one told me you were back." She's looking me over like she can't believe I'm really there. It makes me feel pretty good. "How are you, Remy?" she says.

I tell her I'm fine. I tell her I'm back living with my mother and my sister. But I don't tell her how weird they both act around me and how I feel like a stranger in my own house now.

Then Asia's expression changes. She gets serious and looks a little worried. She says, "You stopped writing to me."

I don't know what to say to that, so I just shrug.

"Are you mad at me, Remy?" she says.

Mad at her? How could I ever be mad at her?

"You wrote me two letters. I was so glad to hear from you. But then you stopped." She hesitates and looks back across the street at Lissa, who's waiting for her. Lissa doesn't look mad anymore. She looks worried, like she's afraid maybe I'll do something to Asia. "You stopped writing to me," Asia says again. I'm sorry now that I did. I didn't think it would be such a big deal to her after the way we left things.

Asia's eyes are brown and warm, like melted chocolate. She's frowning now. "I thought you were mad at me," she says. "You know, about school. I wanted you to write back to me, Remy. I wanted to know what you were thinking and how you were doing. But when you didn't..." She shakes her head, like she's shaking out something she doesn't want to think about. She smiles, but this time it looks like she's forcing it. "Well," she says, "I guess it's like you always said—it's not like we were going to get married or anything, right?"

Lissa calls to her. "Come on. Marcus will be waiting."

"Marcus?" I say.

Asia looks down. "I'm sorry," she says. She raises her eyes to meet mine. "But you stopped writing. And I really like him, Remy. I'm sorry."

I tell her it's okay. I tell her she's right, it's not like we were going to get married or anything. I tell her nine months is a long time, people change. Then I tell her I have to go, I have an appointment. It's not true, but I say it anyway so I have an excuse to walk away. I think maybe if I stop looking into Asia's warm chocolate eyes, the pain will go away.

It doesn't.

Chapter Two

It was my own stupid fault that I got sent away. When I told one of the counselors that, he asked if I was sorry for what I did. I said I was, but I didn't mean it the way he thought I did. He thought I was saying I was sorry for beating up that guy. But I wasn't. I was just sorry I did it when there were people around who could tell the cops everything. And I was sorry I did it when it was still light out. What I should have done was waited and jumped the guy from behind when it was dark. I should have made sure that neither he nor anyone else got a good look at me.

But I didn't. I was too pissed off to wait.

I'm still not sorry I did it. The guy deserved it. After what he said, he totally deserved it. Asia asked me why I'd beaten the guy so bad—but I didn't tell her. I couldn't. Which meant that I couldn't tell anyone else, either. Not that anyone else seemed all that interested. My mother, the cops, my lawyer, even the judge, all acted like they expected it from me. It was like they figured a guy like me, with all the stuff I'd done, would beat on a guy because maybe he looked at me the wrong way or said some stupid thing that set me off. And I guess that last part is true. So what? They can think what they want. The guy had it coming to him—that and more.

Anyway, after I see Asia on the street, I start walking home. But I only go a couple of blocks before I realize that home is the last place I want to be. My mother doesn't want me there. She's tense around me, like she's afraid of what I might do. My sister won't talk to me except to tell me stuff my mother tells her to tell me, like, *Mom says you should take the garbage out* or *Mom wants you to mow the grass*. I look at them in the kitchen together making supper or sitting together on the couch watching TV and talking about whatever program it is, and I imagine how well they must have got along while I was away. So I don't go home.

The problem is, I don't know where to go. I haven't told any of my old friends that I'm back. I'm not sure how they'll react, whether they'll want to see me or not. A couple of them wrote me once or twice, but I didn't write back to them, either. What was there to say? That I hate it here, that there are people in here who are way more messed up than me, that being in here is like being in school 24-7, but with a principal from hell and locks on all the doors? What kind of letter would that be?

And what would I say in the next letter? Nothing ever changed. It was one day after the next after the next. Nothing interesting happened and for sure nothing fun.

So instead of going home, I just walk around. I don't think I'm going anywhere in particular. But I guess my feet have their own plans because after a while I see the schoolyard up ahead and a bunch of guys playing hoops. The guys see me, and a couple of them come out through the opening in the fence that runs around the basketball court. They grin at me—James and Stephen and John—and thump me on the back and ask me when I got home. James says, "Come on and shoot some hoops with us." So I do. And it's okay. It's relaxed. No one asks me questions I don't want to answer about what it was like in there. No one hassles me about what happened. No one even mentions the guy I beat up. We just shoot hoops and have a good time.

We're about to go and get something to eat when some other guys show up. I don't know who they are, but I can tell that the guys I'm with know them. Know them and don't like them. Don't get along with them.

The new guys stand outside the fence. They have a ball with them and I can see that they want to play, but they don't want to play with us. They watch us, and the guys I'm with look back at them. Then, all of a sudden, they start playing ball again. I don't get it. A minute ago they were ready to leave. They were talking about going to a burger joint. But now they're shooting hoops again and making a big deal out of it. It's like they're in some big competition, like the game is gearing up instead of winding down.

I look at James. He says, "No way those guys are playing on *our* court." He doesn't even bother to keep his voice low. It's like he wants the other guys to hear him. And they do. They hear him loud and clear, and the next thing you know, they're inside the fence and everyone is shoving everyone else.

The shoving turns into punching. Someone takes it on the nose and I see blood.

I look around. I don't even know these guys. I sure don't want to fight them. But then two of them are all over James, and I have no choice. I have to help him. That's exactly what I'm doing when the cops show up.

Chapter Three

It's only one cop car. Sometimes it takes a lot more than that to settle things. Sometimes one is enough. Today, one is all it takes. As soon as the other guys see the two uniforms get out of the cop car, they take off running.

"Cowards," James says. There's a cut over his eye. I don't know how it got there, and already that eye is starting to swell shut. "Cowards," he says again as the cops come toward him. One of them is Dunlop, but he's hanging back, letting his new partner make the first move. Well, I guess I'd do the same thing if I were him. The way I heard it, he nearly died that time. If I were him, I would have quit the cops. I would have figured it's not worth it. For some reason, Dunlop didn't quit. But, boy, he sure hangs back.

James doesn't.

James says, "You see those guys who ran? They attacked us. They came here to our court and they attacked us."

He's yelling this at Dunlop's partner, who is so young he looks like he could be Dunlop's son.

"Those—" James stops. I know what he was going to say, and I know why he stops. He wants the cops to lay it all on the other guys, and he's afraid that if he calls the other guys what he was going to call them, the cops will blame him instead of the other way around. My dad, when he was around, used to say there was a time when regular people—by which he meant people who were born here—could count on cops to take their side. He said that wasn't true anymore. He said now they teach cops about crap like diversity. They teach them about cultural sensitivity. He said they recruit those people. The result, he said, is that regular people can't count on cops the way they used to. I guess James knows that. Maybe his dad is like my dad, but I don't know for sure. I never talked to James much.

The young cop looks at James like he doesn't believe him. He says, "Why would those kids attack you?" Really what he's saying is, "What did you do to *make* them attack you?"

Then Dunlop steps up. He looks at James and Stephen and John and the rest of us—it seems like he looks at me the longest—and he says, "The city's changing, boys."

I glance at James. I don't have to be a mind reader to know what he's thinking—No kidding it's changing!

"You better start swimming," Dunlop says. The rest of the guys look baffled.

Who said anything about swimming? But I know what he means because I know a few things about Dunlop. He doesn't mean we should put on our bathing suits and jump into the water. He's just saying that we have a choice, you know, like that old Bob Dylan song. You either swim or you sink like a stone. I think that's how it goes.

Dunlop zeroes in on James. He says, "You want to press charges?"

James laughs. Right. Like getting the cops involved ever made a situation better instead of worse.

"Those guys," he says. "They think they can just take over. But they can't. No way."

The young cop gives us a warning. Fighting never solves anything, he says. Dunlop looks right at me. He knows me—not like a friend, but like a cop. He's stopped me a few times. He even let me off with a warning a couple of times. I bet he's sorry he did. He knows I've been away, and I bet that tells him everything he needs to know about me from here on in.

The cops leave.

James touches his swollen eye and winces. Everyone tells him how bad the eye is going to look later. It will probably swell shut, and the bruise will turn a rainbow of colors before it goes away. James has a smile on his face, but it's phony, not real. After all the kidding dies down, he says, "This is *our* court. Those guys have no right to take it over."

I still don't get it. "What's the big deal about those guys?" I say. "They look like they have play."

"Yeah," James says. "They got play. But they act like they're the only ones who've got it."

He sounds bitter and I try to think why. The guys who were just here are no different from a lot of guys who were in my school before I went away. There were all kinds of guys in my school—probably still are. So what?

"Those guys," James says. "They move into our school and they think they can take over everything."

"What do you mean?" I say.

"I mean, you go down to the courts and they're all there together. Just them, like they're too good for anyone else. They're all like that."

I think, does he know who he's talking to? Does he even remember Asia? But, yes, it turns out he does.

"You know what I'm talking about, Remy," he says. "You saw how Asia's parents were with you."

"That's different," I say. "That was because of all the trouble I've been in."

"Yeah, well, you weren't here," James says. "You don't know what those guys are like. They closed the school near Eastdale." Eastdale is a big subsidized housing project. "So all those kids came to our school. They didn't even try to fit in, Remy. They just hung together. They tried to take over."

"What happened to their school?" I say. What I'm really wondering is, What happened to the basketball court down there? The one in the schoolyard is the only one anywhere near Eastdale.

"They tore it down," James says. "They're building condos or something. It'll be a real improvement, if you ask me."

He looks at me like he expects me to agree with him, so I nod. He can read whatever he wants into it. But I'm thinking about all those kids who live down in Eastdale. Where are they supposed to play ball? I'm thinking, If guys like James freeze them out, no wonder they stick together. How would James feel if our school was torn down and we all had to transfer to the school near Eastdale? I wonder what he would do and who he would hang out with. And I think of Asia.

Then everyone starts to talk about the other guys. Who do they think they are? If they think they can take over, they better think again. That's when I get another picture of how much things have changed in nine months. When James and the rest of them talk about the other guys, their faces get all twisted so that they don't even look like themselves. I wonder if I looked like that when I beat up that guy. I sure was mad enough.

Chapter Four

Two days later, the city feels like a giant steam bath. It's so hot and so humid that the minute I go outside, I'm drenched in sweat. But it's not much better inside. We live in a tiny house with no central air, just one antique air conditioner in the living room window that my mother never wants to put on because the hydro isn't included in the rent and the rates are so high. She's made the point more than once that now that I'm back, there's one more mouth to feed. She's always asking me when I am going to get a job.

It's not like I don't want a job. I'm flat broke. My clothes are all at least a year old. My sneakers have holes in them, and my mother counts out just enough money to buy the cheapest possible pair. I keep the money and head down to the youth employment center instead.

I get pretty much what I expected. I get a bunch of questions—like, how come I don't have any recent experience—and a bunch of looks when I answer the questions. Still, a guy there helps me put together a resume that says I am a hard worker and I learn fast. I tell him references could be a problem. He tells me that the kinds of places that would even take a second look at me are the kinds of places that don't care about references.

It takes a week, but I finally get hired on a trial basis by a contractor who pays me minimum wage to shovel some lady's front yard into a Dumpster. The woman wants her lawn lowered—can you believe it? The guy hires me because I'm strong, I'm cheap, and the job doesn't require me to do anything but sweat to death out there in the sun while I dig. I'm even cheaper than renting one of those little digging machines.

But it's work. And work means money. And money means my mother will maybe get off my back for a few seconds.

By the end of the week, the woman's lawn is a foot and a half lower—level with her driveway, which is just the way she wanted it. The contractor pays me cash under the table because the woman pays him the same way, and the contractor says he can use me again next week. He tells me when and where to show up.

So now it's the weekend. I have money in my pocket. I still need a new pair of sneakers, so I head out to get some—not at a mall, for sure not downtown, but out a ways, at a place James told me about that sells brand-name stuff for prices you wouldn't believe. I score a new pair of really good sneakers for not much more than my mother gave me in the first place, which means that I have enough cash left over to make it through another week without having to ask my mother for anything.

The next day, Saturday, I go down to the courts to see if James and the rest of them are there. They are. We shoot hoops, but it's brutally hot out there and, if you ask me, they're not really into it. James is always looking out beyond the chain-link fence, like he's expecting someone. If he is, he keeps getting disappointed. Finally he says, "Let's get out of here. You want to rent a movie or something?"

We head for the video store. James and Stephen end up in a big argument over what to rent. Me, I don't care. I haven't seen many movies lately, so anything is fine with me, especially since we're going to watch it in James's basement, and James's house has central air.

So while they're arguing, I'm looking

out the video store window. That's when I see her again.

Asia.

She's standing outside. She's looking at something and she's smiling. My heart stops. I remember when she used to look at me like that. When she used to *smile* at me like that. And, boy, I wish I'd never stopped writing to her.

Down deep I know it's a bad idea, but I head for the door of the video store anyway. I step out onto the sidewalk. My eyes are filled with Asia and her hot-chocolate eyes and her warm pink smile. My heart is filled with longing. My memory is filled with the feel of her, warm and soft. My ears are filled with her laughter. Asia loves to laugh. She loves to be happy.

I see that she is happy now. She is smiling, but not at me. No. She's smiling at someone else. Her eyes sparkle as she looks at him. She drinks in his eyes, which are the same deep chocolate color as hers, not blue like mine. His skin is the same as hers too, not pale like mine. I can hardly breathe.

I see her hand, the good one, in his.

I see her smiling at him and only him.

Then he turns around, and I recognize him.

When Asia sees me, she keeps right on smiling, like she's actually happy to see me. She says, "Remy, this is Marcus."

Marcus and I look at each other. I can't tell if he remembers me. My brain isn't working right anyway. All I can think is, After what I did, after why I did it, look at what happened. I think, too, that maybe I was crazy in there, because the whole time I wasn't answering her letters, the whole time I wasn't even reading them, the whole time I was feeling sorry for myself for even being in there, *the whole time*, I would close my eyes and I would see Asia's face and Asia's smile. And when I dreamed at night, I would feel Asia's warm, soft skin. And look what happened.

"Marcus," Asia says. "This is Remy, who I told you about."

Boy, I don't know what she said to Marcus about me, but I'll tell you what—Marcus does not look happy to see me. He doesn't smile at me. I think that might be because he recognizes me, but I'm not sure. Instead of holding Asia's hand, he slips his arm around her waist and pulls her close to him. She doesn't resist. But she does look me in the eye, and I can tell she wishes he wasn't doing it, not while I'm standing right there. Marcus just looks at me like, yeah, he's heard all about me, and the big conclusion he's drawn is that I'm a loser. Well, why not? I lost Asia to him, didn't I?

He still has his arm around her waist when they walk away. Asia turns her head like maybe she's going to look over her shoulder at me. But his lips catch her cheek instead and he kisses her. I turn away.

"Hey," James says. He's coming out of the video store with the rest of them, and I see he has two DVDs, not one—a compromise. "Hey, isn't that one of those guys from the courts?"

"Yeah," Stephen says. "And wasn't that Asia?"

Chapter Five

The next week all I do is work. It's a patio this time, and a lady who likes to stand in her glassed-in solarium at the back of her house and watch every move I make. She never once offers me a glass of water, even though she can see how much I'm sweating. She just stands there, sipping coffee from a big mug and watching me. It's like she's afraid I'm going to steal something or break something. I hear her central air conditioner hum and see that she's wearing a sweater in there, she keeps the house that cold. I sweat and sweat and sweat.

By the end of the day I'm thinking up ways the woman could die—horrible, painful ways. By the end of the week the job is finished and the contractor pays me, again in cash under the table. I see him inside the solarium, chatting with the woman. I see the woman smile at him, even though I did all of the work. She doesn't even thank me when I leave.

But I've got more money in my pocket, and the contractor tells me he has more work for me if I want it. He tells me I'm a hard worker, and then he says, "I took a chance hiring you, Remy. But you were honest with me." He meant that I told him where I had been the past nine months. "I respect that," he says.

I don't know what to say. I guess I'm glad he said what he did. But on the other hand, he does most of his jobs under the table so he doesn't have to pay taxes. In case you don't know it, that's illegal. So who is he to tell me what he respects?

It's Friday afternoon and I've just been paid and I'm heading home. I'm walking down one of the main streets in my neighborhood and I see a bunch of kids, maybe a dozen of them, hanging around on the sidewalk outside a place that sells Jamaican food. Something is going on. I can't tell what it's about, and anyway, I don't care. I don't know those kids. At least, I don't think I do. But then I hear a familiar voice. It's Asia. I'm sure of it.

I approach the kids, but cautiously, because they don't know me and I don't know them, well, except for Asia.

I can see her now. She's standing near the middle of the group. Her body is rigid. She looks angry. She says, "Weapons are stupid. *Knives* are stupid." The person she's saying it to is Marcus, who had his arm around her the last time I saw them together. Now he's standing facing her, and he has something in his hand. It's a knife. He must have been showing it to everyone. Now he flips it shut.

He says, "My business is my business,

not your business." He looks around and I think maybe he's one of those guys who doesn't like to be called out in front of his friends, especially when the person doing the calling out is a girl.

"You think I'm going to be with someone who's stupid enough to carry a knife?" Asia says. And I admit it, I feel this *zing*, because I know Asia when she's talking like that. Suddenly I don't care if I know those guys or not. I move in a little closer.

"Well?" Asia says. She's beautiful. A lot of people think someone that beautiful is just like a picture, something nice to look at, that's all. But Asia is smart too. And she isn't afraid of anyone. She's sure not afraid of Marcus. No, she turns and walks away from him, keeping her head high.

Marcus calls her name. He looks angry when she doesn't turn around, when she acts like she doesn't even hear him. He calls her again, louder this time. Asia keeps walking. Marcus takes a step in her direction, but one of the guys he's with says something and he stops. He watches her go. Then he turns away and he and his friends all go inside the Jamaican place. I follow Asia.

I stay behind her for a couple of blocks. She doesn't turn around even once. When I finally catch up with her, I startle her. Then she surprises me. She bursts into tears.

"What's wrong?" I say.

"It's Marcus," she says. "He's going to do something stupid, I just know it."

Tears are dribbling down her cheeks. I wish I had a tissue to give her, but I don't. She wipes at the tears with the palms of her hands. Some girls look ugly when they cry. Their faces get all red and puffy. But not Asia. She looks sad, but she's still beautiful. I wonder if she ever cried over me. I want to take her in my arms and hold her. I want her to want me to hold her.

Then she says, "Why can't people just get along? Why do they always have to fight?"

Asia doesn't like fighting. She doesn't like violence. When Asia was little—I mean really little—someone tried to kill her. It wasn't even personal. It was what was happening in her country—some people there went around killing other people. Mostly they used machetes. Asia and her parents were lucky. They survived. But Asia lost her left hand. She thinks about that hand a lot.

At first when she asks why people are always fighting, I think that's what she's talking about—how she lost her hand. But then I see the look on her face, and I can't help feeling that what she just said is directed at me, too. Like, why did I have to beat up on that guy? Like, if I hadn't, they wouldn't have sent me away. Like maybe she still cares and that's why she smiles when she sees me. And I feel a little hope.

Then she says, "I don't want anything to happen to him, Remy." She says, "I love him."

I remember the look on Marcus's face when she walked away from him. I wonder if she would love him if she had seen that look.

“It’s the guys he hangs around with,” she says. “They’re always acting like they have something to prove.”

I don’t say anything, even though I know exactly what she means.

“They’ve been hassled by the cops,” she says. “By this one cop in particular.”

Maybe Marcus deserved to be hassled. But maybe he didn’t. Cops have given me a hard time sometimes when I didn’t deserve it.

“They can be like that,” I say. “Sometimes when they see kids, they think trouble.”

“Yeah,” Asia says. “But there’s this one cop. I heard people say he shouldn’t even be on the street. His partner was killed. He was knifed. I heard people say he was affected, you know what I mean, Remy? And Marcus...” She hesitates. She looks at me with those brown eyes, and I remember all the times when those eyes were focused on me—only me.

“What?” I say. “You can tell me.”

“He’s a good guy, Remy.”

I wonder, Did she ever say that about

me? Did she ever tell her parents, *Remy is a good guy*?

"What happened?" I ask.

And there she is, biting the lip I used to bite. Asia always tasted good. I wish I could taste her again.

"They were just fooling around," she says. "You know how guys are."

Yeah, I know.

"Down in the park," she says. "You know, the one where the trains go by."

I know.

"They weren't hurting anyone. They weren't doing anything illegal. They were just fooling around. I guess someone must have complained."

There was a row of houses facing the park. Expensive houses. The kind of houses that are owned by people who like to complain when everything isn't perfect.

"So the cops showed up," Asia says. "There were two of them, including this one guy who I heard was just back at work after, you know."

"After his partner was killed?" I say. "After that?"

Asia nods. "And the cop tells Marcus and his friends that there's been a complaint, that they have to get out of the park right away. And Marcus..." She shakes her head. "He lives in Eastdale," she says. "But he's really smart. So is his brother. His brother is so smart he got a full scholarship to law school. He's a lawyer now. Marcus says he wants to be a lawyer too. He knows a lot, Remy. So he tells the cops that they weren't doing anything wrong. He tells them that it's a public park and it isn't even late at night. He says that they'll be quiet if that's the problem, but that the cops can't legally throw them out of the park."

Maybe Marcus is smart some of the time, I think, but it's hardly ever a good idea to tell cops what they can and can't do.

"The cop, the one who was just back at work, he didn't like that. He told Marcus either he had to clear out of the park or he could go down to the police station on a charge of failure to obey a police officer. He grabbed Marcus by the arm. Marcus reached for his cell phone. It was in his back pocket."

The way she's telling it, it's like she saw what happened. "You were there?" I say.

She nods. "That's how I know he was reaching for his cell phone. He was going to call his brother. His brother always tells him, 'The cops hassle you, you call me as soon as you can.' That's all Marcus was doing. He was going to get his phone out and tell them that his brother is a lawyer and that he was calling him. But that cop, he went crazy. He hit Marcus. It was a big deal. Marcus complained. There was an investigation, but the cop got off. But he's still around and he knows Marcus, and sometimes I'm afraid of what could happen, especially because of the guys Marcus hangs around with. And now Marcus has a knife." Her eyes are hard on me now. "Talk to him, Remy," she says.

"*What*?"

"Talk to him. Tell him what happens when you do something without thinking."

She means, when you do what I did. But what she doesn't know is that I didn't do it without thinking. No way. I did it after I had thought it over and decided that, yes, the guy had it coming to him. The guy deserved it. But I don't tell Asia that. Instead I say, "Why would he even listen to me?"

She knows I have a point, but I can see that she doesn't want to let go of the idea. And that makes me feel bad because it shows me how desperate she is to help the guy she loves. And that guy isn't me.

Asia steps in close to me, so now I can smell her skin and the soap she uses and the stuff she sprays on herself after a shower.

"He knows about you," she says. "I told him."

I wonder what she could possibly have told him. Not the whole story. She doesn't know the whole story. No, all she could have told him was, My ex-boyfriend beat a guy so bad he almost died, and because of that he got sent away for nine months. She could also have told him, Don't let that happen to you.

"Please, Remy," she says.

I can't help myself. I tell her yes. But I can't imagine actually talking to Marcus, doing some kind of scared straight thing with him. And I sure can't imagine him listening.

Then it hits me. Marcus's run-in with Dunlop happened just after he returned to work. I know when that was. I read about it in the paper. Marcus got hassled right after Dunlop went back to work, and Asia was there with him when it happened. I imagine a calendar in my head, and that calendar tells me that what she's described happened after I was gone for maybe three months. It happened when she was still writing me letters, but by then I had stopped reading them. I wonder now what was in those letters. I wonder why she stopped writing. Maybe it wasn't why I thought.

Chapter Six

I go home and shower and change. I pass my mother a couple of times, in the kitchen, in the living room, in the hall. But she doesn't say a word to me until supper is on the table—some kind of casserole with hamburger meat and tomatoes and macaroni, and a tub of coleslaw, plus some bread and butter. My mother serves my sister first. She always does. Then she serves me. She waits until I take my plate from her before she says, "Now that you're working, you should be contributing to the expenses around here."

I look across the table at my sister, who, since I went away, has had a part-time job as a cashier at a fast-food place. I know for a fact that she keeps all the money she makes and spends it on clothes and makeup and movies and music. My sister gives me a blank look, like I'm a stranger sitting there or a boarder she and my mother have been forced to take in.

Then I look at my mother, who is watching for my reaction. I'm convinced she wants me to get mad, to tell her, No way, I'm outta here, I'm taking my hard-earned money and I'm leaving for good. The thought has crossed my mind. But my so-called job isn't a real, full-time job. There's no guarantee the contractor will keep calling me back. So I meet my mother's eyes and I say, "Sure." I reach into my pocket and I pull out the money that the guy gave me just this afternoon. I peel off half of it—*half*!

I want to throw it at her.

I want to stuff it down her throat.

I want to watch her choke on it.

But instead I hand it to her, nice and calm and civilized. And then I sit there, still nice and calm and civilized, and I eat my macaroni casserole and my coleslaw. When I'm finished, I rinse my plate, put it in the dishwasher and head for the door. My mother calls out, "Where are you going?" I don't answer. Why should I?

I go to the basketball court, thinking I'll find James and Stephen and John there. And I do. They're all there, the whole gang. They've staked out the court and they're playing and kidding around. Someone brings some cans of soda. Someone else has some weed. One guy has some music, which is pulsing, pulsing, pulsing, like a heartbeat, magnified and amplified, ba-*boom*, ba-*boom*, ba-*boom*. I smoke some weed, and you know what? For the first time in a long time—for the first time in over nine months—I feel fine. I feel more than fine. I feel happy.

There are girls there too. None of them are as pretty as Asia. Some of them are attached to some of the guys. The rest of them are just hanging out. You can tell they want to be hooked up—well, most of them do. One of them, a dyed blond named Lindsay, starts talking to me, mostly about dumb stuff, like, did I see this movie or do I like this group. She's still at it later, when the game has wound down and someone has gone to 7-Eleven for chips and cakes, and we're eating those and drinking more soda. I smoke some more weed, and before long Lindsay starts to look pretty good. Nowhere as good as Asia, of course, but Asia isn't there.

Lindsay snuggles up against me and slips her hand under my T-shirt. She runs her hand over my chest, then over my stomach. And I can't help it. It feels good. Plus, I've been smoking weed, which is why I lean into her and put a hand on her breast and, well, let's just say I'm glad it's dark in the corner of the court where we are.

It's dark and I'm with Lindsay and her hands are all over me and my hands are all over her. And then, all of a sudden, I'm blinded by a light. It takes me a few seconds to realize it's headlights. I hear car doors open and then slam shut again. James yells out to shut off the lights. So, of course, they stay on. For a while. Then, without warning, they go off and I'm blinking again, this time trying to adjust to the darkness.

When I can finally see again, I make out three guys standing on the other side of the chain-link fence that goes around the basketball court. The one in the middle is Marcus. He's smiling this weird little smile. He's looking at me and at Lindsay. She still has her hands all over me. I shove her away and stand up. I turn to Marcus. I want to tell him that what he just saw doesn't mean anything. I want to tell him—*beg* him—not to tell Asia. But I know if I do that, he'll definitely tell her, just to get back at me. And I hate him for it. I hate Lindsay too. And I hate myself.

James and all the rest of them, even the girls, are lined up on one side of the chain-link fence. Marcus and his bunch are on the other side. Everyone is looking at everyone else. Then one of the guys on Marcus's side of the fence says, "Your time is up."

James goes nuts. He grabs the fence with both hands and jumps up on it and says, "Yeah? Is that so? You want to come over on this side and say that?"

For a moment, nothing happens. Then everyone on Marcus's side of the fence starts to move.

Starts.

And then stops again because there's a cop car sliding up the street. It slows down. Then it stops. Everyone on both sides of the fence backs up a little. James is down from the fence now, but he's staring hard at Marcus. Marcus is staring back. He's delivering a message: Don't screw with my guys. Then he nods and he and his guys get into the two cars they drove up in. They back up and turn, nice and slow. Stephen mutters that they're chickenshit now that the cops are there. But I know that's not it. Not exactly. They just don't want to give the cops an excuse to hassle them. I hold my breath. I hate to admit it, but I'm hoping the cops will make them pull over. I'm hoping they'll hassle Marcus. I'm hoping one of the cops is Dunlop.

The cops don't move. They watch Marcus's car and the other one drive away, still nice and slow. Then they sit there some more, making a point that even James can't miss.

"Come on," he says finally. "Let's get out of here."

We leave the court. James wants to hang out somewhere else. Lindsay is at my elbow, telling me she doesn't know what she did to make me mad, but that she's sorry, really sorry. Which is stupid, right? How can you be sorry when you don't even know what you did wrong? It's kind of pathetic, if you ask me.

I tell her and James that I have to go. I lie and say this guy I've been working for needs me for a job tomorrow. The whole time I'm walking home, I'm thinking about Asia. I'm wondering if Marcus is going to see her tonight. I'm wondering what they're going to do when they're together. I'm wondering what he'll tell her about what he saw. And, most of all, I wonder if Asia will even care.

Chapter Seven

The next day I lie low. I want to tell my mother and my sister, that if anyone calls for me, to tell them I'm not here. But I know that will freak out my mother. She'll think I've done something. She'll think I'm hiding from the cops. So I just stay in my room, out of everyone's way. After a while, my mother knocks on my door to tell me she's going out, she'll be back later, if I want something to eat, I'll have to get it myself. The tone of her voice makes me think she wouldn't care if I starved to death.

The whole time I was away, my mother came to see me exactly once, a week after my birthday. She brought me a present—a CD that my sister must have picked out because it was crap—and a bag of candy. She didn't say much. I think she was embarrassed to have to come there. I bet she never talked about me to her friends. My mother is like that. When my dad took off, she never mentioned him again. It was like she was trying to pretend he never existed. Sometimes I think that's what she has against me. Everyone says I look exactly like my dad. Even I can see it. My sister looks like my mother's side of the family.

Now that I'm back, I can tell she wishes I wasn't. But until I can get something permanent, until I can make enough money, there's nothing I can do about it except stay out of her way as much as possible.

My mother goes out. My sister is at work

all day. And the phone rings. I hesitate—what if it's James? I told him I was working today. If I answer, he'll know I lied.

The phone rings again.

What if it's Asia?

Stupid, I tell myself. Why would it be Asia? Especially if Marcus told her he saw me and Lindsay together with our hands all over each other.

But I still hope she'll call. Maybe she cares.

So I pick up the phone.

It isn't Asia.

It isn't James, either.

It's the contractor I've been working for. He tells me where he wants me first thing Monday morning.

I'm alone in the house, so I go to the fridge to see what there is to eat. Answer: not much. No wonder my mother told me if I wanted something, I'd have to get it myself. She hasn't done the shopping. Maybe she doesn't want to. Maybe she's afraid I'll eat everything she buys. I remember how she used to say, *You're eating me out of house and home.*

I get dressed and walk to the closest pizza place. I buy a slice and a pop and I take them across the street to a little park. I find a bench tucked away in a corner, away from the street, under a big old tree. I sit there and eat my pizza. I wash it down with pop and look at the grass and the flowers. Everything is so peaceful that I sit there even after I've finished my slice and pop. It's cool under the tree, and I like the sound of the leaves rustling in the breeze over my head. Where I am, at the far end of the park, there's a high, thick hedge that runs along the edge of the park, hiding it from an alley and the back fences of a bunch of houses.

I'm still sitting there maybe half an hour later. I'm trying to calculate how much work I will have to do for the contractor who has been hiring me before I have enough money saved up for first and last months' rent somewhere, plus enough left over for food and transportation. Then I start thinking about how much money I would need to buy a used car and how much insurance I would have to pay. I also think about how high gas prices have been. I'm wondering if I'll ever be able to own a car when suddenly I hear a sound. It's feet pounding on pavement.

I stand up.

I look around. Through the hedge I see a guy streak down the alley. He's running like he's being chased by the mother of all grizzly bears and the bear is gaining fast. A moment later, I see why.

The guy *is* being chased—by two cops, both on foot. It's Dunlop and his partner. To my surprise, Dunlop is way out in front. He's pounding after the guy. He's really pouring on the steam until, *boom*, he grabs hold of the guy and jerks him right off his feet.

Dunlop yells at him to lie facedown on the ground and put his arms out in front of him, *straight* out in front of him, palms down, where Dunlop can see them. The guy must be stupid or deaf, or maybe he doesn't speak English, you never know, because he reaches for something instead.

And out comes Dunlop's gun. He points it right at the guy. Dunlop is yelling at him. I mean, he's really yelling, telling him to lie down flat on his belly and put his palms on the ground, *glue* those palms to the ground, *do you hear me?* He's got his gun pointed at the guy. But the guy is still moving around instead of doing what he's told. I look at him and I think I know why he's still moving, but Dunlop either doesn't see it or doesn't care. He screams at the guy again and I hold my breath because it looks to me like Dunlop is going to shoot the guy.

Then Dunlop's partner shows up. He takes a look at what's going on and gets it right away. He puts a hand on Dunlop. He talks to him in a quiet voice. He says, "He's injured. The guy is injured."

I can see it's true. The guy isn't just moving. He's writhing like a snake down there on the pavement. He's got hold of one knee and he's moaning. Maybe he broke it when he hit the pavement. Maybe he wrenched it. It obviously hurts like hell. Either that or the guy is one hundred percent wuss. I get the feeling he doesn't even register Dunlop and his gun.

Dunlop's partner speaks to him again. He tells Dunlop again that the guy is injured. He's got this look on his face, like he's wondering if Dunlop is all there, if he can handle his job anymore. I remember what Asia told me.

Dunlop's partner finally gets Dunlop to holster his gun. The whole time, Dunlop has his eyes glued to the guy on the pavement. Dunlop's eyes are kind of glassy and he's breathing hard. When he finally puts his gun away, he goes over and kicks the guy, hard, in the kidneys. I know what that's about. He's punishing the guy. Not for running. Not for disobeying orders. But for scaring the crap out of Dunlop. Dunlop's partner looks around, like he's afraid someone might be watching. I duck down behind the bushes and stay there until they're gone.

Chapter Eight

It was on the news and in all of the newspapers, what happened to Dunlop. Eighteen years with the police service, all of it as a patrol officer, which I think should tell you something.

He's out one night with his partner. Not the guy he's with now, but another cop, a guy named Andruski. They're patrolling. They're doing their thing. They're the eyes of the night. Crime watchers. Law enforcers. The thin blue line. Whatever you want to call them.

According to the news, they had pulled into the parking lot of a strip mall somewhere in what they call an *under-served* part of town. Supposedly they were observing the area because there had been trouble around there—kids out breaking windows in some of the stores that had been empty for a year or more. It sounded fishy to me. Who in their right mind is going to start breaking store windows with the cops sitting right there? Or maybe that was the whole point. Maybe they were protecting those stores on a crime prevention basis. Maybe they were making a show of force so no one would dare break any more windows.

Anyway, according to the news, which supposedly got its information mainly from Dunlop but also from a witness who arrived on the scene when the incident was almost over, a man appeared in the parking lot. The news said it looked like he was drunk or on drugs or something. He was staggering and weaving. He came right up to the cop car that Dunlop and Andruski were in and pressed his face against the window on the passenger side where Andruski was sitting. The news reports didn't say this, but I imagine this guy with his face up against the window, like a kid looking in a store window when they're doing all the Christmas decorations.

Andruski and Dunlop don't like this, of course. Cops don't like it when people are that close to their cars. They don't like it when people touch their cars. Then the guy smacks the windshield. Andruski and Dunlop *really* don't like that. They get out of the car—Andruski on the side where the crazy guy is, Dunlop on the other side.

The crazy guy—because he'd have to be crazy to do what he's doing, right?—backs up a few steps and starts babbling. That's what the paper said, quoting Dunlop. The guy was babbling. He wasn't making any sense. He was dancing around like a clown too. Dunlop doesn't like it. Andruski, though, he's amused. Dunlop wants to arrest the guy, but Andruski says, Forget it, he's harmless, let's get out of here. He turns his back on the guy and starts to get into the car.

Dunlop told the news, "Andruski shouldn't have done that." He said he shouldn't have done what he did, either, which is that he started to turn away and walk back to the driver's side of the patrol car. He told the news that was when he saw it out of the corner of his eye. He said it was just a flash, the metal catching the beam of a streetlight. He said it took a couple of seconds for it to register—the guy had a knife.

A couple of seconds is also all it took for the crazy guy to swing his knife. Dunlop dove for it. He said later that he shouldn't have bothered. He said that he should have pulled out his gun and shot the guy. But he didn't. No, instead he dove for the knife.

And missed.

Dunlop said it all happened so fast that Andruski didn't understand what was going on until the knife cut him. Some guy they interviewed on the news—I think he was a doctor—said that even if it had happened in a hospital operating room, there was nothing anyone could have done to save Andruski. The knife—and it was a big one, a sharp one—caught him in the upper thigh. It severed an artery. Blood spurted everywhere. Andruski was dead—bled out—in a couple of minutes.

I wasn't there, so I don't know what Dunlop was thinking. But I can imagine what I'd be thinking if I saw someone I knew get stabbed and then have blood spurt out of them like that. I'd be in shock. And I'd be mad. Boy, I'd be mad. And I guess Dunlop was mad too, because he rushed the guy. But he didn't draw his gun. Jeez, I thought that was the first thing cops did. But Dunlop didn't, maybe because he was in shock. He didn't draw his gun. He rushed the guy to try to get the knife away from him, and the guy swung at him too.

Dunlop went down.

Who knows what would have happened if a car hadn't swung into the parking lot at exactly that moment. The guy who drove up said that at first he didn't see anything except a cop car and a crazy-looking guy who turned and ran away. Then he saw someone lying on the pavement. He said he hesitated for a moment. He admitted he was scared. But when nothing happened—I guess he meant when no one shot at him—he got out of his car. He went over to Andruski first. He said he saw right away that he was dead. He couldn't find a pulse. He said he saw another cop lying nearby and he thought he must be dead too. This guy, this passerby, was reaching for his cell phone to call 9-1-1 when Dunlop said, "Tell them there's a police officer down."

They said on the news later that Dunlop was lucky to be alive. His picture was everywhere for a while. So was Andruski's. They had one of those big cop funerals for him, the kind where cops from all over the country show up. They made a big deal when they finally caught the guy who did it. It turned out he really was crazy. He's in some place for crazy killers now. They also made a big deal—but not as big—when Dunlop finally went back to work. If you ask me now, after seeing him with that guy in the alley, Dunlop never should have gone back to work.

Chapter Nine

I spend the next week with two other guys, both older than me, digging, preparing and laying down a massive stone driveway with a sun pattern in the middle of it. The house at the end of the driveway looks like some kind of mansion. It's way out of town, so I have to take the bus to a corner near where one of the guys lives, and he drives me and the other guy there in his pickup. One of the guys, the one with the pickup, hardly ever says a word. The other guy never shuts up. He must watch CNN every minute that he isn't out working because he updates us on every news story, every sporting event, every new movie there is. Plus he gives us his opinions on everything. I can hardly get a word in edgewise, but mostly I don't want to, so it doesn't matter. After a couple of hours that first day, I wish he'd just shut up. It's like working with an all-news radio going full-blast all day. I'm ready to do a happy dance when Friday rolls around again and we get paid and the guy with the pickup drops me off.

After I clean up, I decide to head out to the courts. I haven't been there all week because I have to get up before six every morning, and it's eight or nine o'clock at night when I get dropped off at the bus stop again. So usually I grab a couple of pizza slices or a burger, and then I go home, take a shower and crash. Some life, huh? Some fun summer.

Friday night I'm tired too. But I'm also bored. And you know what? I'm also wondering if Lindsay will be down at the courts. She talks too much, like the guy I've been working with all week. But she has great hands.

So I grab a bite to eat. Then I go home to get cleaned up. By now my mother doesn't bother asking me if I'm staying for supper. She knows I'm not and she doesn't even try to hide her relief. Whatever.

I shower. I put on the new jeans and the new shirt I bought on the way home the night before. And I go out.

I tell myself I'm going directly to the courts, but halfway there my feet take me on a detour. I end up in front of the building where Asia lives. It's a high-rise in a row of high-rises that tower above the street after street of crappy little houses that look even crappier after I've spent a week working outside a genuine mansion. Asia lives on the second floor, middle apartment, around the back, so I walk back there to see if maybe she's out on the balcony. All last summer, when I was still home and still with Asia, she liked to sit out on that balcony, even on steamy hot days. Asia loves summer. She never cares how hot it gets. It never bothers her.

So I go around the back, ready to look up to see if she's there. But it turns out I don't have to look up, because she's right down there at ground level in one of the little courtyards that people who live on the ground floor have instead of a balcony. This courtyard is directly under Asia's balcony. In the courtyard with her are Marcus and a couple of other guys. I watch them for a few minutes from near the corner of the building, and I figure out from who goes in and comes out again that the courtyard belongs to one of Marcus's friends. He lives right there, one floor under Asia. I wonder if that's how Asia met Marcus. Maybe she knows the guy who lives below her, and maybe that guy introduced the two of them.

I feel like a ghost standing there, half-hidden, watching. They're all sitting out on lawn chairs. Asia and Marcus are holding hands. I guess Marcus says something funny because Asia laughs. The sound reminds me of little silver bells, the kind you hear at Christmas. I tell you, everything about Asia is beautiful. Even her laugh.

One of Marcus's friends says something. His voice isn't musical like Asia's. His voice is sharp, like razor blades. I don't know what he's talking about, but his fists come out, *baff*, *baff*, *baff*, like he's pounding something or maybe someone.

Then—I don't know how she does it; I'm hanging back pretty far—Asia spots me. I see her looking right at me. She lets go of Marcus's hand and stands up.

Marcus stands up too. He says something to Asia. Asia points at me. Then she opens the little gate to the courtyard and she comes toward me. Marcus follows her to the courtyard gate and then he stops, which surprises me. His face is wary as he watches Asia walk over to me. She's smiling, which surprises me too. She says, "Did you come to talk to Marcus like you promised?"

I look over her shoulder at Marcus, standing there by the gate to the courtyard. He's smirking at me. Well, why not? He has Asia. I don't.

"You never told me where he lives," I say.

"But you know where to find me."

I'm about to tell Asia that I didn't come here thinking I might find Marcus. But she takes my hand and, just like that, I lose the power of speech. She pulls me toward the courtyard where Marcus is still standing. The other guys are sitting on lawn chairs. They look at each other and then they look at me.

Asia is still holding my hand when she says, "Marcus, you remember Remy?"

Marcus doesn't say anything. He reaches for Asia's other hand, the one that isn't real. Asia looks up at him, and I know what she's thinking. The first time I touched that hand, she almost cried. She said, "Most people try to pretend it isn't there. They try not to look at it." But here's Marcus, holding it like it's real and gently pulling her away from me. He slips an arm around her waist so that he can hold her close. He likes to hold her like that, probably so he can feel the heat of her body. I used to like to hold her like that too.

Asia smiles at him. Then her face grows serious. She says, "Remy wants to tell you something, Marcus."

Marcus gives me a look, like he can't imagine what he and I could possibly have to talk about.

Asia looks at me. "Go on," she says.

I stand there, not saying a word. What does she want me to tell him? Knives are no good? People who carry knives don't believe that. That's why they carry them in the first place, because they believe that knives *are* good.

Asia's eyes are still on me, like she's willing me to start talking. I don't even know how to begin. Then she turns to Marcus.

"Knives are stupid," she says. "Fighting is stupid. Remy knows that. Remy got into a fight. The other guy was badly hurt.

They sent Remy away, isn't that right, Remy?"

The way Marcus is looking at me, I know he already knows this. Asia has told him, maybe more than once.

"Tell him what it was like there, Remy," she says.

Oh.

So that's the part she wants me to tell. It's the part she doesn't know. Well, one of the parts she doesn't know.

I think about it for a moment, and then I say, "It's better to be here than to be there, that's for sure."

"You hang out with those guys at the courts," Marcus says. The two guys behind him, who are sitting on lawn chairs, sit up a little straighter.

"What guys?" Asia says.

"Guys who think they own the place," Marcus says. "Guys just like him." He nods at me.

"I don't hang out with them," I say.

"Right," Marcus says. "Every time I go down there and they're there, you're there with them. But you don't hang out with them."

The two guys on the lawn chairs get up now and come to stand on either side of Marcus, but a little behind him. It makes him look like the leader.

"You tell your friends it's not their court," Marcus says. "You tell them anyone can play there. You tell them *we* can play there. You tell them if they try to stop us, we'll—" He stops and I think, Boy, where he's heading, I've been there.

Asia turns to him. She says, "You'll what?" She sounds mad.

Marcus keeps his eyes directly on me. He reaches into his pocket. Asia watches him. He pulls something out. It glints in the setting sun. I think, It's his knife. Then I hear a chirping sound and I see it isn't a knife at all. It's a cell phone, and he's flipping it open and turning it on, which is why I hear the chirping sound.

"Or I'll call my brother," he says, "and get him to sue your sorry ass."

The two guys behind him laugh. Asia

looks at me, her eyes big, like she's begging me not to get mad. Like she's afraid I will. Like all of a sudden she's sorry she asked me to talk to Marcus. Like she's afraid I'll beat him up the way I beat up the other guy. I never told her why I did it. I wish now that I had, but it's too late. She's still watching me as she draws close to Marcus and slips her arm around his waist. It's a message to me. She's telling me how much it will hurt her if I hurt Marcus. Right then and there I realize how much I hate Marcus, who has the same chocolate eyes as Asia.

I turn and walk away. I hear Marcus and his friends laughing. I tell myself I don't care. But you know what? It isn't true.

Chapter Ten

I never told Asia why I did it because all I could think was how much it would hurt her if she knew. And the last thing I wanted was to hurt her. Also, I was embarrassed to tell her. I was embarrassed to repeat what that guy said to me.

Here's the way I remember it: Asia and I are in the park. It's the one down near the railroad tracks where there's a swimming pool with a slide and a diving board and a big wading pool for the little kids. In winter there's a rink for hockey and another one for just fooling around. There's also a playground for little kids and a lot of big trees that you could sit under on a hot day and still feel cool.

It's near the end of summer, and Asia and I are down there together under one of those big trees. We're hidden away where we're sure no one can see us, and our hands are all over each other and we're kissing each other. Asia tastes sweet.

"Boy," I say, "I wish we didn't have to go back to school next week."

Asia goes quiet. She pulls away from me. She says, "Remy, I have to tell you something."

When people say that, they almost never follow it up with good news.

I wait.

"It's about school," she says.

Asia and I are in the same grade, only she does way better than me at school. She's really smart.

"My parents transferred me to another school," she says.

"What?"

She can tell I'm stunned.

"When did this happen?" I say.

"They were talking about it all last year," she says. "They were bugging me about it. They want me to go to this girls' school. It's supposed to be a really good school. Everyone who goes there ends up in university, a lot of them with a full scholarship."

I'm sitting up straight now.

"I got a scholarship to the school," she says. "It's expensive, but they said at the school that they think I have real potential."

I can see she's proud of herself and that she wants me to be proud too. But all I can think is, If she's going to this school starting next week, then she's known about it for a while. And if it's an expensive school that's given her a scholarship, then she must have applied a while ago and even talked to them a couple of times—otherwise, how could they be so impressed with her? I think she's known about this for a long time, and she's only telling me now.

When I don't tell her how proud I am, she stands up and says she has to go home.

I get up and say I'll walk her.

She says no, and it hits me that she's been saying no for a while. She's happy enough to come out and be with me, but she never lets me go to her house. Usually I don't make a big deal about it. I mean, who wants to be face-to-face with a girl's parents, right? But tonight I tell her I want to walk her home. Especially if she's going to a different school and I won't see her as much.

She says no. She's mad at me. She tells me part of the reason she has to go to this school is because her parents don't approve of me.

I think she's kidding. "What's not to approve of?" I say.

"Because you get into trouble all the time," she says. "Because of those guys you hang around with. My dad says it's bad enough you're—" She stops then, but I know what she means because she gives me a look that reminds me of the look my mother gave me the first time she saw me with Asia.

That time my mother said, "Who was that girl?" When I told her, she said, "Why can't you go out with a normal girl?"

"What do you mean?" I said. "Asia's normal."

"You know what I mean," my mother said.

"No, I don't," I told her, even though I knew exactly what she meant. She and my father think the same way about some things. I told her, "People don't think like that anymore."

My mother looked at me like I was crazy. "Maybe *some* people say they don't think like that, Remy. But don't kid yourself. Most people do. They say they're not prejudiced, but then you see who their friends are and who they marry. People just naturally like to keep to their own kind. They feel more comfortable that way. Besides," she said, "that girl is handicapped."

I told her she didn't know what she was

talking about. I told her Asia lost a hand, that's all. I told her that never stopped Asia from doing anything. I told her, "Asia doesn't think the way you do." I even said, "Asia's parents don't think the way you do," even though I only met them once. But now, in the park with Asia, it looks like I'm wrong. That's exactly how they think. They're sending Asia to a different school—a girls' school—so there's no way she can get involved with anyone like me. And Asia must agree with them, because she's going and she's waited until the last minute to tell me.

"What's their problem?" I say. "We have a good time together, that's all. It's no big deal. It's not like we're going to get married or anything." At the time, I had just turned sixteen. Asia was still fifteen. But I see right away it was the wrong thing to say.

Asia looks at me and says, "You know what? I'm glad I'm going to a new school." She sounds mad and I know it's because of what I said. She turns and walks out of the park. And I'm mad at her, so I don't try to stop her. It's only after she's gone that I see this guy I know, a guy named Shane. He's standing behind me, shaking his head.

He says, "Who does she think she is, huh?"

I'm already mad—at Asia's parents, who want to get Asia away from me; at Asia for going along with them; at my mother for sticking her nose into my business; and now at Shane, who goes to my school but who I don't really know. Who asked him for *his* opinion about *my* life?

"What's it to you?" I say. And it's true, I'm already looking for a way to let off some steam. My hands are already curled into fists.

Shane shrugs. "I'm just saying, that's all."

"Just saying what?"

"Those people," he says. "They're not even born here. They come here and they all stick together. They don't mix with regular people, people like us. They act like they're better than everyone else."

I just stare at him. Part of me wants to tell him he's wrong, Asia's not like that. Besides, it's none of his business. But there's another part of me that thinks Asia's parents sure sound like what he's describing. Who are they, anyway, to decide they don't like me when they don't even know me?

"Besides," he says, "look at her. She has a fake hand. You'd think she'd be grateful that anyone is interested in her. Hey, did you ever see her without that hand? What does it look like? I bet it's gross, huh?"

I know there are other people in the park. I see them, but I don't really see them. Mostly I'm focused on Shane. He's about the same size as me, maybe a little taller. I guess I take him by surprise, because when I hit him the first time, he looks stunned. Or maybe that's because when I hit him the first time, my fist plows into his nose. I see blood. So does Shane. He puts a hand to his face and it comes away dripping red. While he's looking at his bloody hand, I hit him again. And again. And again. Until finally he's on the ground and I'm still pounding on him. I don't stop until he's not moving anymore. And then I'm so tired it takes me a few moments before I realize that the smart thing to do is run.

I go home—fast. I change. I dump the bloody clothes in the garbage out back. It doesn't help. The cops come to the house. They have a positive ID—from someone else, not from Shane. It turns out that Shane is unconscious in the hospital. He ends up staying there for a long time. I get arrested. I go to court. And then I go away. When Asia asks me why I did it, I say the guy was hassling me. I can see she's disappointed by the explanation. I don't tell her what Shane said. I don't tell her how mad I am at myself because now I've gone and made sure that Asia's parents will never like me, will never approve of me.

And after all that, who is she with? She's with Marcus, who has the same color eyes as her and who touches her other hand.

Chapter Eleven

I go directly from the building where Asia lives to the courts, where I find James and Stephen and John and the rest of them. I tell them what Marcus said, minus the part about calling his brother, the lawyer. James listens. He says, "We'll see about that."

Lindsay is at the courts too, along with some other girls. Even though I shoved her away the last time I saw her, she acts like she wants to be with me again. And after what happened at Asia's place, I figure, what the hell. The only thing is, I wish Asia were here to see me with Lindsay. I wish it really bad.

After we leave the courts, we go to James's house. His parents aren't around. I have no idea where they are. We go downstairs to the basement, which is where James lives, and we roll some joints and smoke them and eat chips and order pizza and watch a movie. Don't ask me the name of it. I don't remember. Eventually people start to leave, but I stay. I don't want to go home. I crash on James's floor.

When I wake up the next day, James is sitting cross-legged on his bed, eating cereal and watching TV.

"Hey," he says when I lift my head off the floor. "You hungry?"

I'm not, but I ask about coffee and James goes and gets me some. I drink it and my head starts to clear. James says, "So, what do you want to do today?"

What do I want to do? I want to get Asia back from Marcus. I want to turn back time. I want to correct all my mistakes. I want everything to be different. I want to erase Marcus. More than anything, I want to erase Marcus.

After a while, Stephen comes over. Then John. They say, "Let's go shoot some hoops," and off we go to the courts. We're just rounding the corner when I see James's face change, and no wonder. The court is occupied, and not with little kids, who we could easily shoo away. No, it's Marcus and his friends. There are more of them than I remember. They're all over the court and around it. One of them spots us. Then another and another until no one is playing ball anymore. They're all just standing there looking at us. Marcus's eyes flick from me to James and back to me again.

James starts toward the court. John pulls him back.

"You see how many there are?" he says.

I do. There are way more of them than there are of us.

James shakes John off and steps forward again. He's looking directly at Marcus. He says, "You're on our court."

Marcus looks at the guys on either side of him. He smiles. He's still smiling and he shakes his head when he looks at James again. He says, "How can it be *your* court when you're out there and we're in here?"

I see James twitch.

"We can get more," he says quietly to Stephen and John and me. Then he says, loud this time, "You think you can play here? You're wrong."

Marcus laughs. He isn't scared at all. He thinks James is funny. He probably thinks we're all funny, and why not? He has the court and the manpower to keep it. Which is probably why he says, "You want it? Come and get it."

James has been waiting for this because he has an answer ready. "Tonight," he says. "You want to settle this once and for all, you be here tonight."

Marcus laughs again. Then his face

grows serious and he throws the basketball he's holding. The only reason it doesn't hit James in the face is the chain-link fence that separates us.

James laughs. "Tonight," he says again. He turns around, but slowly, to show Marcus he isn't afraid. He walks back to where we're standing, and we all look at Marcus and his friends. Then, like soldiers in formation, we walk away, still taking our time, still wanting Marcus to get the message—we aren't afraid of him.

We walk back to James's house and hang out on the porch. James starts to make plans. He wants as many guys there tonight as he can get. He wants to show Marcus that he can't take over a court that doesn't belong to him.

Part of me wants to say it's a public court. It belongs to whoever gets there first and it's theirs for as long as they stay. After that it belongs to someone else. But I don't say it because I don't feel like defending Marcus, not when he has Asia. I also don't want James and the rest of them to think that I care more about Marcus than I do about them. I sit on the porch railing, leaning against one of the pillars, and I listen to James talk about who he wants to get out there tonight. He wants guys not to come empty-handed. "You got a baseball bat, bring a baseball bat," he says. "Bring anything you have that you think you can use."

And that's the first time I say it. I say, "Marcus has a knife."

James looks up at me sitting on the porch railing.

"I've seen it," I say. "It's a big one. It looks like it could do some damage."

James's face grows more serious.

"I've heard plenty about those guys," he says. "I heard about them even before they moved into our school. They think they can scare people. They think they can take over. Well, we're going to show them they can't."

Everyone nods.

"What if he doesn't show up?" John says. He's trying to sound as tough as

James, but I can hear in his voice that he's nervous. When a bunch of guys with baseball bats and maybe chains and rocks meets another bunch of guys, and one of them has a knife, who knows what will happen? Who knows who will get hurt?

"If he doesn't show up, he's chicken," James said. "And we win."

And there it is, the look on John's face that tells me what he's hoping for—he's hoping that Marcus and the rest of them won't show up.

We hang around for most of the day. Guys come and go. James orders a couple of pizzas. Everyone gets mellow and I think maybe nothing will happen after all. Maybe everyone will chill out and forget all about Marcus. But as soon as that thought comes into my head, so does a picture—a picture of Marcus and Asia, their arms around each other's waists. I get mad.

It gets late and we're still at James's place, waiting for James to give us the word. It's a hot Saturday night. Guys are drinking sodas. Some guys are drinking other stuff. The sun gets lower and lower. Finally James says, "Let's go."

We walk the ten blocks from James's house to the court behind the school. We're all spread out and we're trying to look casual, like James told us. The guys who have baseball bats are carrying them like they're on their way to a game. Stephen has one. Every now and then he swings it and mimics a home run and lets out a whoop.

The guys who have lengths of chain or rocks they've picked up are more careful. No way guys with chains and rocks look like they're off to a field somewhere to play pick-up ball.

The sun is almost at the horizon by the time we round the corner and catch sight of the court.

No one is there.

I glance at John. He looks relieved. He starts to smile. Then his smile freezes and I turn my head to look where he is looking. Here comes Marcus and he's got a lot of guys with him. A lot.

"Come on," James says. He heads for the other side of the court, where Marcus and his friends are.

John catches him by the arm. "Are you crazy?" he says. "We're outnumbered."

I look around, trying to count how many of us there are and how many of them. Just as I'm almost done, more of us come around the corner. Now it's Marcus's guys who look nervous.

James starts to circle around the fence so he can get to where Marcus is. Guys follow him. They're moving fast, like they can't wait to get there. John hangs back, uncertain. Stephen glances at him, and I guess that's when John makes up his mind. He speeds up so he can join the rest of them. He has a rock—a good-sized one—in his hand and he tosses it up and catches it while he walks. I'm pretty sure he's doing it because his nerves are jangling, but if I didn't know him, I would think he was itching for a fight.

I guess that's what Marcus's guys think too, because someone throws something.

John lets out a scream and sinks to the ground, clutching his eye. After that, things get crazy.

People start running. Our guys rush toward Marcus's guys. Marcus's guys rush toward our guys. Guys are trying to hurt other guys. I mean, really hurt them. And all I can think is what happened last year when I beat up Shane and he ended up in the hospital.

I hang back and I don't care who knows it. I hang back and wait for it to be over. But everything changes when all of a sudden James goes down. Some of our guys run to help him. A few of them look really freaked out when they see that he's bleeding. It looks like someone cut him on the cheek. Maybe someone with a knife. While the guys who are helping James have their backs turned, Marcus's guys rush them. And that's when our guys run.

I turn and see Marcus smiling as half of our guys, maybe more, take off. James is still bleeding, but he yells at them to come back, come back. Marcus stops smiling. More than anything, he looks disappointed. I realize that he doesn't want to fight any more than I do. But James is telling our guys not to run. He's telling them, Look what they did to me, look what they did to John. He's yelling, "Are you going to let them get away with that?" And everything changes again.

Now our guys are rushing Marcus's guys. Our guys with the baseball bats have them held high, our guys with the chains are swinging them, our guys with the rocks are throwing them. More people get hurt. And it turns out, even with how many we have, that it's mostly our guys who get hurt. And they start to run again. They run because when you get hurt like that, with a length of chain or a rock, it isn't exciting like it is in the movies or on TV. You don't just take a blow and then get up and land one on the other guy. You feel it. You really feel it. And you get scared. Is something broken? Am I bleeding? Am I going to die? And if you can, you run.

Even James runs. And I think, This isn't turning out how he expected.

Then I see *where* James is running. He's running into our neighborhood. He's running toward his own street, where all the people are more or less the same, where there are no people like Marcus. That's just the way it is.

Once they're on home turf, our guys start to scatter. They know the houses and the neighbors. People are outside on their porches, and they look alarmed to see their kids and their neighbors' kids being chased up the street by Marcus and a bunch of guys who look just like him. I guess one of them calls the cops, because a car pulls up and two cops get out. I see that it's Dunlop and his partner.

Chapter Twelve

Everyone scatters, and all of a sudden there's just Marcus on the street. Marcus with a rock in his hand, which he is getting ready to throw.

Dunlop's partner says, "Drop the rock." He says, "Drop it now." I see him pull out his gun. He says, "Drop it now and get on the ground, facedown. Now."

Marcus stares at the two cops and I remember what Asia told me. I look hard at him and I see it. Yeah, he must be scared. He's been here before, with Dunlop and his partner, and now he's probably thinking, Shit.

"Drop the rock," Dunlop's partner says.

This time Marcus lets go of it. The rock clatters to the pavement.

"Get down," Dunlop's partner says. "Now."

Marcus is staring at Dunlop's partner and at the gun he's holding. Me, I'm looking around at James and the rest of them, and at all the people on their porches and front lawns. Only a few of Marcus's guys have stuck around. Who can blame them? The ones who haven't run or who aren't hiding are standing way back, ready to take off if they have to. But they don't want to leave until they're sure that Marcus is okay.

"Get down," Dunlop's partner says again.

Marcus lowers himself slowly to the pavement. He's looking around at all the faces on the street, and you can tell he doesn't want to have to lie down on the ground in front of all these people, no way. And you know what? I don't blame him.

But he's down there on the ground anyway. He's got his neck craned up so he can see what's happening. Then something changes. He sees Dunlop. I think he's noticing him for the first time. I think before that, all his attention was focused on the gun that Dunlop's partner was holding on him.

But now he sees Dunlop and suddenly he doesn't want to be lying down there anymore, letting himself get handcuffed by Dunlop's partner and then put into the back of a police car. No way.

I remember what Asia told me.

I know that Marcus and Dunlop know each other and that Dunlop is going to be tough on Marcus.

Dunlop's partner has one knee on Marcus's back. He's pulling one of Marcus's hands around behind Marcus so that he can cuff him. But Marcus isn't lying there taking it anymore. Marcus is trying to get up. He's fighting to get up. I'm standing close enough that I hear him say one word: lawyer. I see something glint in his hand, the one that Dunlop's partner hasn't got hold of yet. I know what Marcus is doing. I know what's in his hand.

I see Dunlop turn around. I see him look at Marcus struggling. I hear him say, "What the—"

Marcus's hand, the one that's still free, comes up and around. That's when I yell, "He's got a knife!"

Marcus's hand, the one that's holding something, hits Dunlop's partner on the shoulder. Dunlop yells at his partner, "Down!" Then he shoots, *bam*, *bam*, *bam*—three times. Marcus isn't moving anymore. The cell phone drops from his hand.

It's quiet. Everywhere it's quiet, even though, when I look around, I see that an even bigger crowd has gathered. There are all kinds of people now—people from the neighborhood and people from outside the neighborhood.

I see Asia.

She's looking right at me, right through me, right into my heart, and I can see that she knows what I've done. She stares at me. I see the disappointment in her eyes. And the hatred. It rips into my heart. I want to go to her. I want to explain. I want to lie—I thought I saw a knife. Then I want to tell the truth. But I do neither. Instead I watch Asia walk over to the cops—not Dunlop and his partner, but the ones who have just arrived. I watch her talk to two of them. I see her turn and point at me.

The next time I see Asia is maybe six months later, after the inquiry that clears Dunlop of the shooting. I told them there that I knew Marcus had a knife. I told them I thought he was reaching for it, I was sure I saw it. I told them it was an honest mistake. James and Stephen and John back me up—they say they knew that Marcus had a knife. James even says he was pretty sure he saw it. I wasn't there when it happened, but I know they asked Asia too. And Asia had to tell them he had a knife. She had to tell them it was true that she worried about him because of the knife.

After the inquiry is over, I come out of school one day and there Asia is, standing down on the sidewalk. My heart races. She walks up to me and I can see that under her coat she is wearing a school uniform. I smile at her. She doesn't smile back. Then I say what I always wanted to say. I say, "I didn't read your letters." I tell her exactly why I didn't and that I'm sorry. I say, "I thought it was over, because of your parents."

"I wrote to tell you that I love you," she says. "I wrote to tell you that no matter what my parents think, I love you."

I want to wrap my arms around her. I want to kiss her.

But she steps away from me. "I came to tell you, Remy, that I know. I know what you did. I know you lied at the inquiry. I can't prove it, but I know."

Her eyes don't remind me of warm, sweet chocolate anymore. She stares at me, and then she turns and walks away.

I watch her until she is gone.

I want to turn back time. I want to correct all my mistakes. I want everything to be different. But it's too late.

Norah McClintock has written a number of titles in the Orca Soundings series including the best-selling *Tell* and *Snitch*. Norah lives in Toronto, Ontario.

Orca Soundings

Bang
Norah McClintock

Battle of the Bands
K.L. Denman

Blue Moon
Marilyn Halvorson

Breathless
Pam Withers

Bull Rider
Marilyn Halvorson

Bull's Eye
Sarah N. Harvey

Charmed
Carrie Mac

Chill
Colin Frizzell

Crush
Carrie Mac

The Darwin Expedition
Diane Tullson

Dead-End Job
Vicki Grant

Death Wind
William Bell

Down
Norah McClintock

Exit Point
Laura Langston

Exposure
Patricia Murdoch

Fastback Beach
Shirlee Smith Matheson

Grind
Eric Walters

The Hemingway Tradition
Kristin Butcher

Hit Squad
James Heneghan

Home Invasion
Monique Polak

House Party
Eric Walters

I.D.
Vicki Grant

Juice
Eric Walters

Kicked Out
Beth Goobie

Orca Soundings

My Time as Caz Hazard
Tanya Lloyd Kyi

No More Pranks
Monique Polak

No Problem
Dayle Campbell Gaetz

One More Step
Sheree Fitch

Overdrive
Eric Walters

Refuge Cove
Lesley Choyce

Responsible
Darlene Ryan

Saving Grace
Darlene Ryan

Snitch
Norah McClintock

Something Girl
Beth Goobie

Sticks and Stones
Beth Goobie

Stuffed
Eric Walters

Tell
Norah McClintock

Thunderbowl
Lesley Choyce

Tough Trails
Irene Morck

The Trouble with Liberty
Kristin Butcher

Truth
Tanya Lloyd Kyi

Wave Warrior
Lesley Choyce

Who Owns Kelly Paddik?
Beth Goobie

Yellow Line
Sylvia Olsen

Zee's Way
Kristin Butcher

Orca Currents

Camp Wild
Pam Withers

Chat Room
Kristin Butcher

Cracked
Michele Martin Bossley

Crossbow
Dayle Campbell Gaetz

Daredevil Club
Pam Withers

Dog Walker
Karen Spafford-Fitz

Finding Elmo
Monique Polak

Flower Power
Ann Walsh

Horse Power
Ann Walsh

Hypnotized
Don Trembath

Laggan Lard Butts
Eric Walters

Manga Touch
Jacqueline Pearce

Orca Currrents

Mirror Image
K.L. Denman

Pigboy
Vicki Grant

Queen of the Toilet Bowl
Frieda Wishinsky

Rebel's Tag
K.L. Denman

See No Evil
Diane Young

Sewer Rats
Sigmund Brouwer

Spoiled Rotten
Dayle Campbell Gaetz

Sudden Impact
Lesley Choyce

Swiped
Michele Martin Bossley

Wired
Sigmund Brouwer

Orca Sports

All-Star Pride
Sigmund Brouwer

Blazer Drive
Sigmund Brouwer

Cobra Strike
Sigmund Brouwer

Hitmen Triumph
Sigmund Brouwer

Hurricane Power
Sigmund Brouwer

Jumper
Michele Martin Bossley

Kicker
Michele Martin Bossley

Rebel Glory
Sigmund Brouwer

Tiger Threat
Sigmund Brouwer

Titan Clash
Sigmund Brouwer

Two Foot Punch
Anita Daher

Winter Hawk Star
Sigmund Brouwer

Down